MW00528235

Kodachrome

by Adam Szymkowicz

SAMUELFRENCH.COM   SAMUELFRENCH.CO.UK

FOR PRODUCTION ENQUIRIES

UNITED STATES AND CANADA
Info@SamuelFrench.com
1-866-598-8449

UNITED KINGDOM AND EUROPE
Plays@SamuelFrench.co.uk
020-7255-4302

Each title is subject to availability from Samuel French, depending
upon country of performance. Please be aware that *KODACHROME*
may not be licensed by Samuel French in your territory. Professional
and amateur producers should contact the nearest Samuel French
office or licensing partner to verify availability.

MUSIC USE NOTE

Licensees are solely responsible for obtaining formal written permission from copyright owners to use copyrighted music in the performance of this play and are strongly cautioned to do so. If no such permission is obtained by the licensee, then the licensee must use only original music that the licensee owns and controls. Licensees are solely responsible and liable for all music clearances and shall indemnify the copyright owners of the play(s) and their licensing agent, Samuel French, against any costs, expenses, losses and liabilities arising from the use of music by licensees. Please contact the appropriate music licensing authority in your territory for the rights to any incidental music.

IMPORTANT BILLING AND CREDIT REQUIREMENTS

If you have obtained performance rights to this title, please refer to your licensing agreement for important billing and credit requirements.

KODACHROME was developed in the Dorothy Strelsin New American Writers Group at Primary Stages in New York, New York. It was workshopped at JAW: A Playwrights Festival, produced by Portland Center Stage in Portland, Oregon in 2015.

KODACHROME had its world premiere at Portland Center Stage in Portland, Oregon; Chris Coleman, Artistic Director. It opened February 9, 2018. It was directed by Rose Riordan with sets and lights by Daniel Meeker, costumes by Alison Heryer, sound by Casi Pacilio, projections by Will Cotter, and original music composed by Jana Crenshaw. The production stage manager was Janine Vanderhoff. The production assitant was Jordan Affeldt and casting was by Brandon Woolley and Rose Riordan. The cast was as follows:

PHOTOGRAPHER............................... Lena Kaminsky
POLICEMAN /
    HARDWARE STORE OWNER .... Ryan Vincent Anderson
GRAVEDIGGER / YOUNG MAN .... Ryan Tresser
LIBRARIAN / WAITRESS / FRIEND .... Tina Chilip
HISTORY PROFESSOR /
    PERFUME MAKER / EMT 1................... John D. Haggerty
MYSTERY NOVELIST / FLORIST / EMT 2 .... Sharonlee McLean
MARJORY / YOUNG WOMAN .... Kelly Godell

CHARACTERS

5-16 total
3f, 2m up to 8f, 6m, 2 gender neutral
Actors can be any race

PHOTOGRAPHER – (mid-30s to mid-40s) Suzanne, female
GRAVEDIGGER – (mid-30s to mid-40s) Earl, male
HARDWARE STORE OWNER – (mid-30s to mid-40s) Charlie, male
HISTORY PROFESSOR – (early 60s) Harold, male
MYSTERY NOVELIST – (early 60s) Georgette, female
MARJORY – (mid-20s) Female
YOUNG MAN – (early 20s) Robert, male
YOUNG WOMAN – (early 20s) Florence, female
FRIEND – (early 20s) Female
EMT 1
EMT 2
LIBRARIAN – (mid-30s to mid-40s) Renee, female
WAITRESS – (early 30s to mid-40s) Jen, female
PERFUME MAKER – (early 30s to mid-40s) Martin, male
POLICEMAN – (early 30s to mid-40s) Pete, male
FLORIST – (mid-30s to mid-40s) Heather, female

Doubling for 5

Gravedigger / Young Man / Policeman
Hardware Store Owner / Perfume Maker / History Professor / EMT 1
Mystery Novelist / Librarian / Florist / Friend / EMT 2
Young Woman / Waitress / Marjory

Doubling for 7

Gravedigger / Young Man
Hardware Store Owner / Policeman
Librarian / Waitress / Friend
History Professor / Perfume Maker / EMT 1
Mystery Novelist / Florist / EMT 2
Marjory / Young Woman

SETTING

Colchester, Connecticut
a small rural New England town

TIME

The present or recent past

NOTE ABOUT PROJECTIONS

These are not entirely necessary. I think the photographer just showing the audience is also effective in an *Our Town* kind of way. Which is to say please don't be daunted by the projections. They are nice but entirely unnecessary.

If you do projections, I suggest the photos taken onstage be taken beforehand in actual locations like an actual diner or an actual library so there's a richness that you won't be able to get from an onstage photo. In the original production, they were projected onto the rear wall.

For the photos of the audience, in Portland, the actress had a wireless video transmitter connected to her camera and concealed in her costume. They used a program called Isadora to "watch" the video feed from the camera, and output individual frames of the feed to a projector as the actress took photos. They found that outputting a video feed from the camera and capturing images on the computer eliminated the delay incurred by outputting images from the camera directly. Again, if that seems daunting, just have her take photos which aren't projected.

SPECIAL THANKS

In no particular order to Rose Riordan, Chris Coleman and the amazing staff, cast and crew at PCS. Don and Mary Blair, Tim and Mary Boyle, Keith and Sharon Barnes, Ronni S. Lacroute, Kelly Douglas and Eric H. Schoenstein, Ritz Family Foundation, John and Rhoda Szymkowicz, Seth Glewen, the Gersh Agency, Tish Dace, Kristen Palmer, Wallace Szymkowicz. Tom Cleary. Elizabeth Bochain. Joe Kraemer.

Moritz von Stuelpnagel, Michelle Bossy, the Primary Stages Writing Group, Project Y Theatre. The JAW team: Susan Louise O'Connor, Danny Wolohan, Gavin Hoffman, Sharonlee McLean, Laura Faye Smith, Karin Magaldi, Maria DiFabbio, Kelly O'Donnell.

Jason Schlafstein and the cast and crew of the workshop he directed at The National Conservatory of Dramatic Arts in DC: Nan Kyle Ficca, Phil Da Costa, Doug Wilder, Britney Mongold, Cambria Ungaro, Briyan Moreno, Camella Maloney, Antonio Sellers, Vitaly Mayes, Natalie Boland, Matthew Baldoni, Marketa Nicholson, Maria Paz Lopez.

Lia Romeo and the 17-18 Project Y Theater writing group: Rae Mariah MacCarthy, Daaimah Mubashshir, Stephanie Swirsky, Stacie Lents, Nora Sorena Casey, Holly Hepp Galvin, Pia Wilson, Dan B Moyer, Alexis Roblan, Tyler Dwiggins.

At Juilliard: Tony Meneses, Brian Watkins, Donja Love, Morgan Gould, Tearrance Chisholm, Krista Knight, Madhuri Shekar, Jonathan Payne, Jenny Rachel Weiner, Jessica Moss, Marsha Norman, David Lindsey-Abaire. Richard Feldman, Kathy Hood, Jerry Shafnisky, Sarah Wells, Kaitlin Springston, Brittany Giles-Jones, James Gregg, Lindsey Alexander, Thomas Cline.

Marya Mazor and the cast and crew at Saddleback College: William Francis McGuire, David Anderson, Kent McFann, Tim Swiss, Lynn Durgom-McQuown, Chris Canada, Michelle Macdougall Jackson, Michael McCormick, Kristina Savage, Michael Ouimet, Jimmy Carlsen, Cole Altuzarra, Sarah Halasz, Jayden Leacock, Joanna Weingartner, Mikayla Kotlensky, Becca Orsbern, Ashleigh Gerberry.

Gwydion Suilebhan, the New Play Exchange, and all those who left reviews there of this play: Aleks Merilo, Gina Femia, Mike Sockol, Kat Ramsburg, Emma Goldman-Sherman, Ben Rosenblatt, Rachel Carnes, Ian August, Claudia Haas, Elenna Stauffer, Mark Mason.

Special thanks to the many, many actors who helped me by performing in development readings of this play.

For all those who live or have lived in Colchester, CT.

For love.

For you.

ACT I

Scene One
The Photographer

(Projected: inhabitants and environs of a small town. But something is a little off. A little odd. The color saturated and too dark. The camera too close. Unusual perspective. Things like that.)

*(During the slideshow, the **PHOTOGRAPHER** enters. She is in all white or in muted colors and she wears a camera around her neck. She smiles at us.)*

PHOTOGRAPHER. I have loved! – No. Let me start again.

   (Beat.)

I take photos. It's important, I think, to record things. To remember how things are right now. Later, people will want to know. Will wonder and think about days past. So I take a lot of photos of everywhere and everyone here in town. I'm not an official photographer although there are political grumblings from time to time to that effect. Does a town need an official photographer? Or an official poet? An official dreamer? An official lover? If the casual is made official, would that stop the rest of us from dabbling? That would be a crime in itself. So I don't need to be the official photographer. But I am good at it. People always come to me for keepsakes, or for help remembering. 'Course I'm having a bit of trouble remembering now too. Little things. It's one of the side effects of my condition. I'm getting ahead of myself. I take photos. I can't stop time so instead I – I have photos up in a lot of public spaces. For historical record. For art, maybe. I don't know if it's art. I just help people look at things. Sometimes. If they're open to it. You can call me Suzanne. Or the Photographer. Hold on.

(*Raises her camera to her eye, takes photos.*)

Stay still. Yeah. Turn your head just. You're very photogenic. You too. Show me your sadness. Good. A smile? A sad smile. Now joy. Great! Can you button that up?

(*The* **PHOTOGRAPHER** *takes a bunch of photos of the audience. They appear on the screen behind her.*)

Good. That's great. I want to remember this. Maybe you will too. So. If you need anything, probably I'm the one to ask. Anything within reason I mean. Within my control. I'm not sure what's within my control. Where to first? Our time is limited.

(*Spot on the* **PERFUME MAKER** *in lab coat mixing scents. The* **PHOTOGRAPHER** *takes a photo and it is projected on the back wall.*)

The Perfume Maker makes perfume.

(*He smells it.*)

PERFUME MAKER. No. It needs more... This. No. This. No. Ah-ha!

(*Lights on* **YOUNG WOMAN** *and* **YOUNG MAN**.)

PHOTOGRAPHER. The Young Man thinks about the Young Woman. The Young Woman thinks about the Young Man.

(*They steal a glance. Lights out on* **YOUNG WOMAN** *and* **YOUNG MAN**.)

(*Spot on the* **LIBRARIAN**, *walking.*)

The Librarian walks by the hardware store on the way to the library. She wills herself not to look in the window.

LIBRARIAN. I will not.

> *(Lights up on* **HARDWARE STORE OWNER** *with pipe.)*

PHOTOGRAPHER. The Hardware Store Owner does not see her walk by. He is measuring a length of pipe and trying not to think about the hole in the center of him he hasn't been able to fill.

HARDWARE STORE OWNER. And seven eighths.

> *(Spot on* **GRAVEDIGGER.***)*

PHOTOGRAPHER. The Gravedigger looks at the sky and wonders if it will rain.

GRAVEDIGGER. I wonder if it will rain.

PHOTOGRAPHER. He scans the gravestones looking for ghosts, but he sees none.

> *(***GRAVEDIGGER** *sighs. The* **PHOTOGRAPHER** *takes a photo and it is projected on the back wall. Lights on* **HISTORY PROFESSOR** *and* **MYSTERY NOVELIST.** *She is writing while walking. He is reading.)*

The History Professor and the Mystery Novelist both enter the kitchen at the same time from different directions. They both reach for the coffee pot.

> *(This happens.)*

HISTORY PROFESSOR. You go ahead.

MYSTERY NOVELIST. No, no. You.

HISTORY PROFESSOR. I insist.

> *(They freeze. Lights out on them.)*

> *(Lights on* **YOUNG WOMAN** *and* **YOUNG MAN.***)*

PHOTOGRAPHER. The Young Man thinks about the Young Woman. The Young Woman thinks about the Young Man.

> *(They steal a glance. Lights out on* **YOUNG WOMAN** *and* **YOUNG MAN.***)*

(*The* **FLORIST** *enters.*)

PHOTOGRAPHER. The Florist opens her flower shop.

FLORIST. Another day.

PHOTOGRAPHER. She is optimistic.

FLORIST. I think. Yes. I think. Why not?

> (*The* **PHOTOGRAPHER** *takes a photo which is projected. Lights on* **PERFUME MAKER** *at table.*)

PHOTOGRAPHER. The Perfume Maker sits in the diner at his regular table. "Today," he thinks.

PERFUME MAKER. Today.

PHOTOGRAPHER. The Waitress sees him come in. But she does not get up yet. She does not reach for a menu, not that he would need it. In a minute she'll get up. Or two.

> (*The* **WAITRESS** *sips coffee. The* **PHOTOGRAPHER** *takes a photo and it is projected on the back wall.*)

PERFUME MAKER. Today –

PHOTOGRAPHER. He thinks.

WAITRESS. Another day.

PHOTOGRAPHER. She thinks.

> (*Lights up on the* **LIBRARIAN**.)

PHOTOGRAPHER. When the Librarian stops in the grocery store before lunch, there the Hardware Store Owner is, looking at radishes.

> (*Spot on* **HARDWARE STORE OWNER**, *examining a radish.*)

She ducks behind the heads of lettuce.

> (**LIBRARIAN** *hides. The* **PHOTOGRAPHER** *takes a photo and it is projected on the back wall. Lights on* **YOUNG WOMAN** *and* **YOUNG MAN**.)

The Young Man thinks about the Young Woman. The Young Woman thinks about the Young Man.

(They steal a glance. Lights out on **YOUNG WOMAN** *and* **YOUNG MAN.***)*

Have you been to Harry's Place yet? It's a local landmark. We'll go there, yes?

Scene Two
The History Professor and the Mystery Novelist

(Projected: photo of Harry's Place. An older couple sit at a picnic table or rustic outdoor table, the **HISTORY PROFESSOR** *and the* **MYSTERY NOVELIST**.)*

PHOTOGRAPHER. Harry's Place, established nineteen twenty. Drive-in, takeout, affordable hot dogs, burgers and fries. The History Professor and the Mystery Novelist sit in the shade. It's a mild August afternoon. The History Professor fiddles with his wedding ring.

HISTORY PROFESSOR. So.

PHOTOGRAPHER. He says.

MYSTERY NOVELIST. Yes.

PHOTOGRAPHER. She says.

HISTORY PROFESSOR. I guess it's time.

MYSTERY NOVELIST. No point in denying it.

PHOTOGRAPHER. She takes a bite from her lobster roll. Butter drips down her chin.

HISTORY PROFESSOR. I'll have it all drawn up.

PHOTOGRAPHER. She smiles at this, a small smile. A slight breeze. They watch a hummingbird pass.

> *(**PHOTOGRAPHER** takes a photo of her, projected on the back wall.)*

MYSTERY NOVELIST. I do appreciate, of course, your sense of humor.

HISTORY PROFESSOR. Humor?

MYSTERY NOVELIST. Irony. Finality. History? I see how you are rounding it out, putting up bookends as it were.

PHOTOGRAPHER. He thinks for a moment of the oak bookcase in his study crammed with Civil War tomes. He never liked bookends but he appreciates her appreciation.

HISTORY PROFESSOR. Our first date.

MYSTERY NOVELIST. Yes. You wore a letter jacket. How did you ever letter in anything?

HISTORY PROFESSOR. It was out of pity. You were cold. Wearing a tiny dress. I draped it over you.

PHOTOGRAPHER. She remembers the moustache he tried to grow. He thinks of her seventeen year old legs. They settle into an unsettled silence. That was then. But now – now –

HISTORY PROFESSOR. I'll move into the cottage.

MYSTERY NOVELIST. No, no.

HISTORY PROFESSOR. I insist.

PHOTOGRAPHER. He says goodbye in his mind to his oak bookcase and the red couch in his study. She feels the pull of the novel she's writing. How to get her heroine out of the water. Do boats just come along? Does she float for a while? Was she perhaps a champion swimmer? Reminds herself to look up how long it takes for hypothermia to set in. Instead what she says is –

MYSTERY NOVELIST. What will we tell the kids?

HISTORY PROFESSOR. Jonathan will take it in stride. But Marjory. I worry about Marjory.

PHOTOGRAPHER. She doesn't tell him that Marjory already knows. Over the phone. Last week. Marjory pleaded. Marjory cried.

(**MARJORY** *appears in spot, in pain.*)

MARJORY. Mother, please. Don't do this. He loves you. You love him.

MYSTERY NOVELIST. It wasn't enough.

MARJORY. Are you fighting?

MYSTERY NOVELIST. No. No.

MARJORY. I don't understand.

MYSTERY NOVELIST. I long for an empty bed. I want to drink coffee alone in the morning. I want to be lonely.

MARJORY. Is he having an affair? Are you?

MYSTERY NOVELIST. No. No. I want him to move out before I begin to hate him. His toenails. His breath. The grunty way he stands up.

MARJORY. Don't do this. Please!

MYSTERY NOVELIST. We will be civil when we see you. It is all very civil. We will come visit together maybe. We will have dinner. We will smile and we will enjoy each other's company. How's your roommate?

PHOTOGRAPHER. And Marjory is distracted for twenty minutes talking about the trials of life in Boston and the HR game. She might switch companies. It is what people do, to get ahead, to climb the ladder and ascending is what it's all about, right? But it would mean leaving her team who she has grown fond of. And starting over with new people and new processes.

MARJORY. Do you think I'm ambitious enough? It's something I want to be true about me. But sometimes I can't tell the difference between what I want and what I think I should want. What do you think?

PHOTOGRAPHER. And then she becomes aware of how dull she must sound to her mother, how unartistic, how grounded. Her mother admires her daughter with her feet on the ground, but then there never is the clouds of the mind to discuss. That much they don't share. But the Mystery Novelist asks questions to show she is listening. Like –

MYSTERY NOVELIST. How is the transition to the new software? How did you feel about last quarter?

PHOTOGRAPHER. And Marjory knows her mother is trying. Did she try in her marriage? Marjory cries and pleads and cries.

MARJORY. Noooo!

PHOTOGRAPHER. She feels sorry for herself and imagines she now comes from a broken home. She looks at the bean bag chair and remembers when her parents helped her move in. Was there tension that day? She's not sure. She makes microwave popcorn and falls asleep to *Casablanca*.

(MARJORY exits. Light change.)

MYSTERY NOVELIST. I'll tell Marjory.

PHOTOGRAPHER. She says to her still husband. And a weight he didn't know was there is lifted off his shoulders.

HISTORY PROFESSOR. I'll say something to Jonathan.

PHOTOGRAPHER. And like that, the plan becomes all too very real.

HISTORY PROFESSOR. I'll leave tonight. Pack a few things. Next week, I'll come for more.

MYSTERY NOVELIST. There is no rush.

PHOTOGRAPHER. She says. But doesn't mean it.

MYSTERY NOVELIST. How is your burger?

HISTORY PROFESSOR. It's good. They're always good.

PHOTOGRAPHER. He thinks of Gettysburg. Maybe this year he'll make the reenactments. Where did that tin cup go? He thinks of the student with the short skirt in the front row of History One O One. He looks at his soon to be ex-wife. He fiddles with his wedding ring.

HISTORY PROFESSOR. Supposed to rain later. I'll leave tonight.

PHOTOGRAPHER. She feels the relief of his impending departure. She is able to better taste her food now. It doesn't stick in her throat. It melts. She savors it. His lips are chapped and the ketchup stings just a little.

MYSTERY NOVELIST. I need to stop at the pharmacy on the way back.

PHOTOGRAPHER. She doesn't say, "On the way home." It is a house they no longer share. Let's move on.

Scene Three
The Young Couple

(Projected: photo of the gazebo. The Town Green. The **YOUNG MAN** *and the* **YOUNG WOMAN**.*)*

PHOTOGRAPHER. The Young Couple go for a stroll. She does not realize it is more than a stroll. But she senses something stirring in him, unfamiliar. She says nothing. He is upset perhaps, anxious. This makes her nervous. Is he angry at her? A misunderstanding? Did she speak too sharply earlier when she was hungry and irritable? She can't remember what she said. He is unaware of the tempest in her mind. He has an important question to ask. He reaches into his pocket to feel the ring box. By trickery he got her best friend to find out her ring size.

(**FRIEND** *appears in spot, a ring in her hand.*)

FRIEND. Try this one on. That looks good on you.

PHOTOGRAPHER. The Young Woman did not suspect. Even now, she thinks his silence means the opposite. He is done with her, she thinks. She has always suspected she was not one of those girls who could be loved.

YOUNG MAN. Florence –

PHOTOGRAPHER. He says.

YOUNG MAN. Florence.

PHOTOGRAPHER. She waits for more but the words get stuck in him. She waits for him to say, "It's not working out," or, "We're just too different." "I love you but sometimes love isn't enough." Or something like that. She doesn't know he really wants to say, "I love you madly." "I want to marry you." "Let's spend our lives together." Or something along those lines. He is having trouble getting the words out. He can't speak. He is paralyzed. His throat constricts.

YOUNG MAN. ...

YOUNG WOMAN. Are you okay?

YOUNG MAN. ...

PHOTOGRAPHER. The Young Man begins to hyperventilate. He falls to one knee, thinking she will understand.

(*Takes photo which is projected.*)

YOUNG WOMAN. What is wrong? Can you breathe? Are you allergic to something? Did you swallow something.

YOUNG MAN. ...

PHOTOGRAPHER. She calls nine one one.

YOUNG WOMAN. (*Into phone.*) Something is wrong. Something is terribly wrong.

(**YOUNG MAN** *collapses. She goes to him.*)

PHOTOGRAPHER. He is unconscious when the EMTs arrive.

(**EMT**s *check vitals, give him oxygen.*)

EMT 1. What was he doing right before?

YOUNG WOMAN. I don't know. He fell to one knee. He was breathing too fast.

(**EMT 1** *and* **EMT 2** *nod sagely to one another.*)

EMT 1. I've seen this before. Sir, can you hear me?

YOUNG MAN. Eh...anh...

EMT 2. Shall I check your pocket, sir?

PHOTOGRAPHER. The Young Man nods to the EMT.

(**EMT 2** *takes the ring box from his pocket, gives it to* **YOUNG WOMAN.**)

EMT 2. I believe this is for you.

PHOTOGRAPHER. It gets eerily quiet as the Young Woman has eight separate feelings. One. Two. Three. Four. Five. Six. Seven. Eight.

YOUNG WOMAN. I – I –

(*The* **YOUNG WOMAN** *throws her arms around the* **YOUNG MAN.**)

EMT 1. I think that's a yes.

PHOTOGRAPHER. The Young Man finds his voice again. It had been in the ring box the whole time.

YOUNG MAN. Florence! Will you –

YOUNG WOMAN. Yes, Robert. Of course, yes.

> (*She takes the oxygen mask off and kisses him.*)

PHOTOGRAPHER. Young love. Mmm.

Scene Four
The Gravedigger and the Hardware Store Owner

(**PHOTOGRAPHER** *in spot.*)

PHOTOGRAPHER. I have to – I have to run some errands. I'm sorry. I'm not deserting you. It's just – I won't be long. Just – here is the graveyard. It all comes back here, doesn't it? We try to avoid it, don't we? But none of us...anyway – the Hardware Store Owner.

(**PHOTOGRAPHER** *exits.*)

(*Projected: photo of the graveyard. The* **HARDWARE STORE OWNER** *stands by a grave. He looks down at it, dour. Says nothing.*)

HARDWARE STORE OWNER. So. Um. So. Sometimes it's hard to start. I wanted to say something. I wanted to ask. I have a question, sort of or a something I'm wondering about. But I don't know how. So. Um.

(*The* **GRAVEDIGGER** *enters, stands beside him.*)

GRAVEDIGGER. You didn't bring flowers.

HARDWARE STORE OWNER. No, I.

GRAVEDIGGER. You used to bring flowers.

HARDWARE STORE OWNER. They just die.

GRAVEDIGGER. Oh but. Sure but. Why is that a problem? I have some. I could put down some for her, make her part of the rotation. The Millers got some Thursday but they can wait until next Friday and I could add her. Or maybe there will be more flowers this week. It's hard to control. I go into people's gardens sometimes and pick flowers. Nobody ever says anything. I try not to take the ones that are too pretty, that I know the owners need around. Like the – what do you call them – with the – the – you know –

HARDWARE STORE OWNER. ... Uh...

GRAVEDIGGER. But I think she should still get flowers. I take them away, you know, when they die.

HARDWARE STORE OWNER. I'll bring some next time.

GRAVEDIGGER. Flowers are nice.

HARDWARE STORE OWNER. I'll bring some next time.

GRAVEDIGGER. Sometimes I get the leftover ones from the florist. Before they die but at the end of the day. She likes flowers doesn't she? I think she likes flowers.

HARDWARE STORE OWNER. The florist?

GRAVEDIGGER. No.

    (Beat.)

You want a minute? With the grave? Sometimes people want a minute but they don't know how to tell me.

HARDWARE STORE OWNER. No, that's okay. I have to go anyway.

GRAVEDIGGER. It's okay that you didn't bring flowers. And it's okay if you don't want to say anything. I'll let her know you stopped by.

HARDWARE STORE OWNER. What?

GRAVEDIGGER. She's not here now but I'll let her know you stopped by.

HARDWARE STORE OWNER. Okay. Okay, Earl. Thanks.

GRAVEDIGGER. There's something she's been trying to build up the courage to say. Soon, maybe. I don't know. Everything in its own time. That's what they say. But. There's not much time.

HARDWARE STORE OWNER. Okay. Tell your mother I said, "Hi."

GRAVEDIGGER. I will do that. I will. Looks like I might have to cut the grass early this week. But maybe I'll wait. If there's a grave to dig today, no sense in cutting the grass. You think anyone died? I hope not. It never ends. But not every day, so there's that. Lunch. Maybe I'll have lunch. What time is it? Is it too early?

HARDWARE STORE OWNER. Okay, Earl. You take care.

    (HARDWARE STORE OWNER *exits.)*

GRAVEDIGGER. I don't care if it is too early.

(**GRAVEDIGGER** *gets a cooler / lunchbox. He sits down and starts eating. The* **PHOTOGRAPHER** *appears.*)

GRAVEDIGGER. There you are. He was just here. Your husband.

PHOTOGRAPHER. My widower. He's harder to remember. His edges are fuzzy. Does he seem like he's fading to you?

GRAVEDIGGER. I don't know about that. I'm just saying he was here. He was hoping to talk to you, I think. But he can't hear you. Not like me.

PHOTOGRAPHER. When was the last time you shaved?

(*She takes his photo. It appears on the back wall.*)

GRAVEDIGGER. Please don't do that. I don't like having my photo taken.

PHOTOGRAPHER. I'm sorry. I forgot.

GRAVEDIGGER. You always do that. I don't like it.

PHOTOGRAPHER. I said I was sorry.

GRAVEDIGGER. Okay. I'm going to pick up some flowers for your grave tomorrow. You like flowers, don't you?

PHOTOGRAPHER. Yes.

GRAVEDIGGER. I thought so. Is there a particular kind you like or don't like?

PHOTOGRAPHER. Peonies?

GRAVEDIGGER. I don't know what that is.

PHOTOGRAPHER. I will treasure whatever you get.

GRAVEDIGGER. You don't mind that they die?

PHOTOGRAPHER. No. Everything dies.

GRAVEDIGGER. Yeah, I don't know why that would be a problem either. Everyone likes flowers. It's something nice I can do.

PHOTOGRAPHER. It is.

GRAVEDIGGER. Some things I can't do. But I can do that. So. I do that.

PHOTOGRAPHER. Everyone appreciates it, Earl.

GRAVEDIGGER. Okay. I really like spending so much time with you. I know you don't have a lot of choice.

PHOTOGRAPHER. That's not true.

GRAVEDIGGER. I like having you around I mean. It's been – I'm not good with words, but –

PHOTOGRAPHER. I know. It's nice to talk to you too.

GRAVEDIGGER. Right. That's all I meant. It's been nice. But you know, eventually, one of these days, you will have to move on. It's the natural way and I don't know about a lot of things but I know about the natural way. Say what you have to say to him and then, well, I'll miss you of course and all. You understand what I'm trying to say, right? Does this grass look long to you?

> *(She looks at it. He takes out a tape measure and measures the grass. She takes a photo of him. He freezes. She talks to us.)*

PHOTOGRAPHER. I'm sorry I didn't mention before I was dead. Does it matter too much to you? I still have a perspective. But this isn't about me. It's about them. I'm pretty sure. This is Earl. Five facts about Earl. One. Earl can see and hear ghosts. Two. Earl's father died when he was five. No one ever talked to him about it. It took three more years until Earl realized his father who tucked him in each night was no longer alive. Three. People pity Earl. They forget him. They don't think much of him or think of him much. Four. Earl lives in fear of a sentient robot uprising. Consequently he shuns technology, owns no phones or computer, refuses to drive any car made after nineteen eighty-five. Five. Earl is deeply, madly, and totally in love with me and has been since second grade. Earl is having a lot of feelings right now.

> *(**GRAVEDIGGER** unfreezes. He seems disoriented. Then he finds himself.)*

GRAVEDIGGER. I'll get some flowers for you. The most beautiful ones I can find. Even if it hurts someone to lose them.

PHOTOGRAPHER. Don't do that on my account.

GRAVEDIGGER. Even if it hurts someone.

> (The **PHOTOGRAPHER** *walks away from him towards the diner now being established.*)

PHOTOGRAPHER. I'm not going to say any more about that part.

Scene Five
The Waitress and the Perfume Maker

PHOTOGRAPHER. At the diner.

> (*Projected: interior of the diner. The* **PERFUME MAKER** *sits at a table. The* **WAITRESS** *smokes, a little ways away, apparently in front of the diner.*)

This diner has had twenty, maybe twenty-five different owners, and with the owners, different names. It is hard to keep count. People stopped bothering to learn the new name. "The diner," they say. Or, "The diner across from the Green." "That diner, you know, right there on Main Street." "Near Gung Ho." The Waitress, it seems like, has worked in every version of this diner since it has been a diner. She feels tired enough to have been working there since the town was established – but that was 1698 so of course, no that can't be true. And of course she is young. Is she young? She is ageless. The Perfume Maker sips his coffee. The Waitress has refilled it at least six times so far.

PERFUME MAKER. Today.

PHOTOGRAPHER. He thinks.

PERFUME MAKER. Today. After another cup of coffee.

PHOTOGRAPHER. The Perfume Maker has something to say but he is not used to saying things to people. He works alone in silence. When he works, he looks up and he hasn't eaten. He looks up and he hasn't slept. The Perfume Maker likes to work. He creates new scents and sells them to companies that make perfumes and sometimes lotions and sometimes bath gels or soaps. His nose is valuable and his abilities are more valuable. He is terrible at everything else. The Waitress is a good waitress. The Waitress is not terrible at everything else.

> (*The* **WAITRESS** *puts out her cigarette and comes back into the diner.*)

WAITRESS. Everything okay?

PHOTOGRAPHER. She says. But she thinks –

WAITRESS. Why are you still here?

PERFUME MAKER. I want to touch you.

PHOTOGRAPHER. He thinks. But out loud he says –

PERFUME MAKER. Fine. Fine.

PHOTOGRAPHER. And stares at his coffee cup. The Perfume Maker comes to the diner for lunch every day. He sets three alarms so that he will not miss lunch.

WAITRESS. Need anything else?

PERFUME MAKER. No. No. The fries are good today.

WAITRESS. *(Not listening.)* Yup.

PHOTOGRAPHER. You know that thing when you recognize in another, a spark of something – something you are not and can never be and you want to possess this spark? Some want to crush the spark out, others want to feed it 'til the spark becomes a flame and then the flame becomes an inferno. The Perfume Maker sees this spark in the Waitress. But he doesn't know the words to say this.

PERFUME MAKER. Good fries.

*(The **WAITRESS** refills his coffee cup.)*

PHOTOGRAPHER. The Perfume Maker recognizes the scent the Waitress has behind her ear. He knows the lotion on her hands, the shampoo she used this morning. He smells the fried food from the kitchen, some ketchup spilled some hours ago, and somewhere underneath all that noise, the scent that is her and only her. He breathes deeply. He is overcome. He tries to tell her something.

PERFUME MAKER. I wanted to – can I – um...

WAITRESS. What?

PERFUME MAKER. A spark that when – in the dark – like a small fire –

WAITRESS. What?

PERFUME MAKER. I mean – you. For example. When I smell you –

WAITRESS. When you smell me?

PERFUME MAKER. No. I mean. Not – I'm not –

PHOTOGRAPHER. The Policeman enters the establishment.

> (*The* **POLICEMAN** *enters. The* **WAITRESS** *comes alive. Her posture transforms. She smiles, giddy.*)

WAITRESS. Why hello there, stranger.

POLICEMAN. Not so strange.

WAITRESS. What's this? Two times in one week.

POLICEMAN. It's the coffee. No one makes coffee like you do.

WAITRESS. It's all in the wrist.

POLICEMAN. We could use a wrist like that on the force.

WAITRESS. I think I'm much and much too much for your police force to handle.

POLICEMAN. I can't argue with that.

> (*The* **POLICEMAN** *sits. The* **WAITRESS** *pours him coffee.*)

PHOTOGRAPHER. They laugh. They laugh. She touches his arm.

> (*This continues to happen but silently. The* **PHOTOGRAPHER** *takes a picture of them, which is projected.*)

PHOTOGRAPHER. The Perfume Maker has ugly feelings, but they are feelings he knows he has no right to have. He tries not to feel these feelings. He thinks of a smell that will make him feel hope.

PERFUME MAKER. Lilac. Coriander. Cinnamon. Spearmint. Coffee.

PHOTOGRAPHER. He takes a deep whiff of his coffee.

PERFUME MAKER. I will make her a perfume.

PHOTOGRAPHER. He thinks. A scent just for her, so beautiful she will understand everything he wants to say but cannot figure out how to say. The scent will do it all.

PERFUME MAKER. The scent.

PHOTOGRAPHER. He says nothing to the Waitress. Instead, he leaves much too much money and exits without anyone noticing.

Scene Six
The Florist and the Young Woman

(Projected: interior of the flower shop. The **YOUNG WOMAN** *looks at a binder of bridal bouquets. The* **FLORIST** *stands nearby.)*

PHOTOGRAPHER. The Young Woman is not someone to waste time. Here she is picking out her bridal bouquet.

YOUNG WOMAN. Not this one. No. No. No. It must feel inevitable. It must feel like forever.

PHOTOGRAPHER. The Florist is always a little misty when the brides come in. Each year they get younger and younger and the Florist gets older and older.

FLORIST. It doesn't matter. It's fine.

PHOTOGRAPHER. She thinks.

FLORIST. It will be me next year.

PHOTOGRAPHER. And a wave of anxiety overtakes her. What if? What if not? What if tomorrow? What if never? She can almost taste those lips, can almost smell... But not now. She's at work.

FLORIST. Do you have a color scheme?

YOUNG WOMAN. I just want perfection.

FLORIST. Of course. What time of year? Different season, different flowers.

YOUNG WOMAN. Yes, of course. There are decisions to be made. I guess. I don't know. It has to be right. You understand?

PHOTOGRAPHER. The Young Woman is feeling constricted. She is having trouble breathing. The Young Woman does not understand the tides within her, the eight separate emotions that change into eight other slightly different emotions. One Two Three Four Five Six Seven Eight. One Two Three Four Five Six Seven Eight. The Florist feels the dull pain in her chest that will make her try harder later, but now just makes her ache. She feels this and only this and barely registers the Young Woman.

YOUNG WOMAN. Are these all the options?

FLORIST. There's another book.

YOUNG WOMAN. I need to see all the books. If it can't be perfect, why do it at all?

FLORIST. Love?

YOUNG WOMAN. What?

FLORIST. Because of love.

PHOTOGRAPHER. The Florist thinks about love, about need, about loneliness. She wants to equate love with not being lonely but she knows that can't be right. She thinks of the smells. She wonders what it is to be a tortured genius.

YOUNG WOMAN. Love. Love.

PHOTOGRAPHER. The Florist thinks of a certain individual and tries not to think of this certain individual.

YOUNG WOMAN. It just has to start the right way. What if – do you have suggestions?

FLORIST. Of course. What would you like?

YOUNG WOMAN. No. No. No. You're not helping me at all. I need to get some fresh air!

PHOTOGRAPHER. The Florist has seen this before and is unfazed. The Young Woman runs out of the flower shop. She has never felt this way before. Outside she doesn't feel any better. The Florist feels immediately better. She knows what she must do. She must –

FLORIST. Yes.

PHOTOGRAPHER. The Young Woman does not know what to do.

YOUNG WOMAN. I will go to a different flower shop. In Salem. In East Haddam. In Old Lyme. In Moodus. In Deep River. In Chester. In Hadlyme. In East Hampton. In Cobalt. In Portland. In Middletown. In Chester.

PHOTOGRAPHER. The Young Woman thinks of the anti-anxiety pills in the very back of her sock drawer. But why should she need this, now at the happiest moment of her life? The Florist smiles with a renewed optimism. The flowers die a little with every passing second.

Scene Seven
The Librarian and the Young Man

(Projected: exterior of the library.)

PHOTOGRAPHER. Cragin Memorial Library, built 1905, a fine example of early twentieth century Neoclassical architecture. No one talks about Dr. Cragin much. Not like they talk about Pierpont Bacon. Or Stephen Austin. Or Jonathan Coulton. Although I guess everyone will be forgotten eventually.

(Projected: interior of the library.)

The Librarian looks up at the light bulb that has gone out.

LIBRARIAN. Darn.

PHOTOGRAPHER. It's easy enough for her to put in an order. But there is an account at the hardware store and it's important to support small businesses. She could of course send someone else to get it. But she has been meaning to stop and say hello to the Hardware Store Owner. She's been intending to do so for the last two years. It's about time. She imagines how easy it would be to walk through those doors. This is the part of her that imagines a braver version of herself. Tomorrow she will be thinner, the lines will disappear from her face, she will clean the bathroom thoroughly and she will go to the hardware store. But why not now? Every day it's tomorrow and tomorrow and tomorrow.

LIBRARIAN. Tomorrow.

PHOTOGRAPHER. She's been tomorrowing in one way or another for the past twenty years. Best not to think about it. There are always books to put away. There is knowledge. And imagination. And then the Young Man appears.

YOUNG MAN. Hello.

PHOTOGRAPHER. He says. And –

YOUNG MAN. Excuse me. Sorry to bother you.

PHOTOGRAPHER. And.

YOUNG MAN. I'm wondering if you could help me.

LIBRARIAN. Of course.

YOUNG MAN. I'm looking for a book.

LIBRARIAN. You've come to the right place.

YOUNG MAN. Of course there is the computer, but I was hoping you would know better, being how you are an expert and all and how you know how to find things.

LIBRARIAN. I will do my best.

YOUNG MAN. I am looking for books on marriage. How to have a good marriage. What to do. What not to do. How to be a good husband. How to love the right way. How to best make love. Not fiction, mind you. Or the things on the internet. More like old knowledge. The things our souls know that long ago were shared by word of mouth generation after generation and then recorded by hand and translated into a thousand languages but have been forgotten. Maybe some of the new science too. But not based on one small study and not pseudoscience and not a series of essays written on deadline by someone who doesn't know enough, who knows how to write but doesn't know how to think. Also. How to be a good father. Not the trends. Not the sexism. Or maybe some of the sexism but the kind in which it is easily recognized as such. How to be a good person. How to live life the right way. I feel like I'm trying to start my life finally with the right person and I want to try not to make too many mistakes and I want to be happy or if not happy, the other thing that we're supposed to be. Of use? Worthwhile? Honest? I want to be vulnerable and love completely. Do you have a book like that?

LIBRARIAN. Let me see.

PHOTOGRAPHER. The Librarian is quietly astonished by the Young Man.

LIBRARIAN. I should be more like him.

PHOTOGRAPHER. He worries he has said too much. Perhaps he could have found it all on the internet or in the online catalog. While he worries, she hands him a stack of books.

(*The* **PHOTOGRAPHER** *takes a photo as the* **YOUNG MAN** *accepts the stack of books from the* **LIBRARIAN**. *It is projected*.)

LIBRARIAN. Here. There are more maybe. This is a good start. Come back after you've read these. I will think on it more.

YOUNG MAN. Thank you.

LIBRARIAN. Of course.

YOUNG MAN. I really appreciate it. Really – I thanks!

(**YOUNG MAN** *exits with a large stack of books*.)

PHOTOGRAPHER. The Librarian takes a deep breath.

(**PHOTOGRAPHER** *takes a photo of* **LIBRARIAN** *which is projected*.)

LIBRARIAN. Vulnerable. Love completely. Well. Well.

PHOTOGRAPHER. She feels something rising in her. Inspiration? A call to action? She will not tomorrow today. She will today today. She takes a deep breath. She steels herself.

LIBRARIAN. I'll be back in a few.

PHOTOGRAPHER. She yells to her assistant. And she puts one foot after another towards the hardware store where my former husband is right then ordering hammers.

(*The* **LIBRARIAN** *exits*.)

Let's let her go. We'll catch back up with her later. A word about the Hardware Store Owner. He has been slipping from my memory, piece by piece, like a mirror shattered on the day of my death. I drag him around losing more and more of him all over town. Yesterday, it was pieces of our honeymoon. What color was the sand? Was there a jellyfish or not? I'm forgetting

breakfasts. Oatmeal, maybe bran flakes. A joke about a
donkey whose meaning is lost. His mother's name. The
size of his hands. Every day he is more and more like
a character from a novel I read. A fictional story I'm
forgetting and can never read again. Does he have gold
fillings? Was there an instrument he could play? Even
the love is fading as it expands. I love him because he
is human and less because he is he. Maybe because I
am less and less me. It is a symptom of my after-death.
But enough. More life. More things to see. Pity does not
become me.

Scene Eight
The Florist and the Perfume Maker

(Projected: interior of the PERFUME
MAKER's *lab.* PERFUME MAKER *works. The*
PHOTOGRAPHER *enters.)*

PHOTOGRAPHER. The Florist raps on the door of the
Perfume Maker's house slash lab slash office slash
bachelor pad slash pigsty.

(FLORIST enters, taps on his door.)

The Perfume Maker is working, of course.

(PERFUME MAKER does not look up.)

PERFUME MAKER. Like this? *(Smells.)* No. No. Not for her.
Must be special. Like her. More. Electric. It must take
the more that is she and make it more still.

PHOTOGRAPHER. He imagines the Waitress's scent. He
breathes deeply.

(The PERFUME MAKER *breathes deeply. The*
FLORIST *knocks. This upsets him.)*

PERFUME MAKER. *(Quietly.)* No. No. Not now.

(The PERFUME MAKER *puts in ear plugs.)*

FLORIST. Perhaps he does not hear me.

PHOTOGRAPHER. The Florist knocks louder.

FLORIST. *(Knocking louder.)* Hey! Hi! It's me. Hello!!

(The PERFUME MAKER *looks up.)*

PERFUME MAKER. Perhaps she will go away.

PHOTOGRAPHER. He thinks.

FLORIST. It's me! Hello! Are you there?! Hello! Hello!
Helloo!!!

PERFUME MAKER. I'm busy!

PHOTOGRAPHER. But he is always busy. She will not be so
easily dissuaded.

FLORIST. I will not be so easily dissuaded.

PHOTOGRAPHER. The Florist knows the value of persistence. She does not know her own value but she understands the value of not giving up.

FLORIST. It's just. I have flowers.

PERFUME MAKER. Leave them.

FLORIST. Yes, of course. I can leave them. It's just – I thought...maybe I could give them to you. You could put them in water. So they don't expire.

PERFUME MAKER. *(To himself, but not quietly.)* Expire.

FLORIST. Isn't that a funny word?

PERFUME MAKER. I'm busy. My work is very important. I can't stop now. Must not get distracted. I can't "chat" now. I can't smell your flowers and tell you about them. It's very important. It's life or death.

FLORIST. I know. I just thought –

PERFUME MAKER. I can't. Not now. I have this talent given to me and it's all that I have and I must. I must use it.

FLORIST. I understand.

PHOTOGRAPHER. The Florist says. But she does not understand. And in not understanding, she romanticizes it. She smells her wrist. On it she wears a scent of his she bought at the mall in a store she wouldn't otherwise go into. She paid much more than she had ever paid before for a perfume. She finds the smell intoxicating. It's delicate, like rosewater but more persistent. She feels like royalty when she wears it, or like her idea of royalty. And she feels the longing then too.

FLORIST. His work. It is so important.

PHOTOGRAPHER. She thinks.

FLORIST. It's of such value to the world, what he makes. He is everything and I am nothing.

PHOTOGRAPHER. This way of thinking is dangerous.

FLORIST. I'm nothing.

PHOTOGRAPHER. This is one of the great tragedies of our time. Yet it is so common as to be mundane.

PERFUME MAKER. When she smells it, she will realize and she will see my value, my contribution.

PHOTOGRAPHER. This too is dangerous.

PERFUME MAKER. The scent is out there. Not this, but almost. It has to be perfect.

PHOTOGRAPHER. The Florist is sick of perfect.

FLORIST. I'll just leave the flowers here then. Put them in water as soon as you can.

PERFUME MAKER. Mmm hmm.

PHOTOGRAPHER. He agrees. But he will forget and will not see them even when he once again leaves his house to have lunch at the diner. She will not give up so easily. She will be back tomorrow. And the next day and the next. He has opened his door to her before and surely will do so again, won't he? Of course, he has not yet invited her in.

FLORIST. Persistence.

PHOTOGRAPHER. She says.

FLORIST. Persistence.

PHOTOGRAPHER. Should I say something about that? You understand.

(The **FLORIST** *exits. The* **PERFUME MAKER** *works.)*

Scene Nine
The Librarian and the Hardware Store Owner

(Projected: interior of the hardware store.
HARDWARE STORE OWNER *is there working.*
The **PHOTOGRAPHER** *enters.)*

PHOTOGRAPHER. So. Here we are. If I'm honest, I have to admit I've been avoiding this place. Recently. But here we are. The hardware store. The Librarian lurks outside.

(Enter the **LIBRARIAN** *who lurks.)*

She thinks about entering.

LIBRARIAN. It's just a light bulb. It's no big deal.

PHOTOGRAPHER. She reaches for the door handle. The Hardware Store Owner looks up. Their eyes meet.

HARDWARE STORE OWNER. Oh.

LIBRARIAN. I –

HARDWARE STORE OWNER. Renee.

LIBRARIAN. Charlie.

(They are frozen.)

PHOTOGRAPHER. She should have expected this. But then – there is history, isn't there? How many years ago? Stack one decade upon another. Is that about right? A few years here. A few years there. Perfect. A prom. In the gymnasium in the high school named after Pierpont Bacon.

(A mirrored ball is lowered from the ceiling.
Music. Lights change. The **HARDWARE STORE**
OWNER *and The* **LIBRARIAN** *come together.*
They slow dance.)

The prom theme was "Parisian Nights." The prom song was "In Your Eyes," by Mr. Peter Gabriel. I'm here too. But you can't see me. But I see them. We all do. They are closer than they've ever been. Closer even than later that night when physically they are closer still.

PHOTOGRAPHER. She thinks about the future. Their colleges are not so far away. Weekends together. Maybe some weeknights. And then, graduation, marriage, children. She thinks of names for their kids.

LIBRARIAN. Sophie. Liz. Margaret.

PHOTOGRAPHER. He thinks about later that night. He must be careful. There is a basketball scholarship on the line. College is the way out, the way to say no to the family business. What does he know about screws, drills, viscosity. He thinks about later that night. He presses against her.

HARDWARE STORE OWNER. Nuts and bolts.

PHOTOGRAPHER. Many other boys wish they were dancing with her. Many would like to clean his clock, knock his block off, sock his jaw. Many girls, me included, want to get lost in his arms.

They want to shame her. Erase her. Stuff her in a well. But these two – they are blissfully unaware.

LIBRARIAN. This night is perfect.

HARDWARE STORE OWNER. Yes.

LIBRARIAN. I can't wait for everything that comes next and also I want it to just be now forever, you know what I mean?

HARDWARE STORE OWNER. Yes.

PHOTOGRAPHER. He does know what she means. She hugs him tighter. He smells her hair. It seems like maybe, just maybe this moment will last forever.

> (**PHOTOGRAPHER** *takes a photo of them which is projected.*)

But it doesn't.

> (*The lights change. The* **HARDWARE STORE OWNER** *and the* **LIBRARIAN** *move away from one another. The present day awkwardness returns.*)

LIBRARIAN. Hello.

HARDWARE STORE OWNER. Long time no see.

LIBRARIAN. Busy over there at the library.

HARDWARE STORE OWNER. Here too. You know how it is.

LIBRARIAN. I sure do. Busy.

HARDWARE STORE OWNER. Busy. You wake up and wonder what day it is.

LIBRARIAN. What month.

HARDWARE STORE OWNER. What year.

LIBRARIAN. Right.

HARDWARE STORE OWNER. Exactly. What can I do for you?

PHOTOGRAPHER. Immediately he feels like he said too much.

HARDWARE STORE OWNER. I meant, what can I do for you?

PHOTOGRAPHER. That's not it either.

HARDWARE STORE OWNER. I mean, you need something?

LIBRARIAN. Me? What would I need?

HARDWARE STORE OWNER. I didn't mean to imply. I thought. You were here. Maybe you want. A drill? A socket wrench? Nuts and bolts?

LIBRARIAN. Oh! Oh. Light bulbs. For the library.

HARDWARE STORE OWNER. Of course. Light bulbs. Light bulbs.

PHOTOGRAPHER. The Hardware Store Owner goes to the computer and looks up the type of lightbulbs the library usually orders. He knows where they are and what kind but he goes through the motions.

LIBRARIAN. Do you want the account number?

HARDWARE STORE OWNER. Sure.

PHOTOGRAPHER. He says, even though he has the account number memorized.

LIBRARIAN. Zero Six Four One Five, Eight Six Zero, Two Zero Three, Eight, Six Seven Six Seven Seven Seven, Two Two One Five Three Eight Seven Two Three Nine One One Seven Six.

*(You don't have to memorize this number.
Keep saying numbers. If they laugh, say one
more number after the laugh. If not, just stop
eventually. Always end on one.)*

LIBRARIAN. One.

HARDWARE STORE OWNER. Got it.

LIBRARIAN. I like those light bulbs.

HARDWARE STORE OWNER. They're really good. We sell them
a lot.

PHOTOGRAPHER. This isn't really the conversation either of
them wish they were having right now. How did we get
here? Two weeks after the prom there was a fight.

(Lights change. The **LIBRARIAN** *and the*
HARDWARE STORE OWNER *fight.)*

Who can say what it was really about? Fear of the future.
Loss of control. Worry. The problem of independent
personalities.

LIBRARIAN. You're just like your father!

HARDWARE STORE OWNER. You're like your mother!

LIBRARIAN. You're a stubborn jerk!

HARDWARE STORE OWNER. You're mean!

LIBRARIAN. Stop looking at me with those stupid eyes in
that stupid face.

HARDWARE STORE OWNER. What do you know about it?

LIBRARIAN. You're a selfish slob!

HARDWARE STORE OWNER. You don't ever understand me!

LIBRARIAN. You don't understand me.

HARDWARE STORE OWNER. I wish I never had to deal with
you ever again.

LIBRARIAN. Then maybe we should break up.

HARDWARE STORE OWNER. Maybe we should.

(Lights change.)

PHOTOGRAPHER. It was never supposed to happen. Or it
was never supposed to last long. When I asked him

out, he said yes to make her mad. Probably. I wasn't supposed to get pregnant. Definitely.

We got married right away. Quickly, quietly. Days turned to weeks. Weeks turned to love.

HARDWARE STORE OWNER. Love.

PHOTOGRAPHER. He turned down his scholarship. He took over the family business. The future Librarian went to college. And then my baby came and she was stillborn. We mourned. Instead of driving us apart, we grew closer together. After two more miscarriages, we stopped trying. The future Librarian came back from college and got a job at the library. And then life and life and life. Until four years ago when I came down with bone cancer and then two years ago when I stopped being alive.

> *(Lights. Back to present.)*

LIBRARIAN. You find it?

HARDWARE STORE OWNER. Incandescent. I'll have them for you in a minute.

LIBRARIAN. I've been meaning to stop by and say hi anyway.

HARDWARE STORE OWNER. Sure. Hi.

LIBRARIAN. Hi.

HARDWARE STORE OWNER. How you doing?

LIBRARIAN. Good. You?

HARDWARE STORE OWNER. Good.

PHOTOGRAPHER. He can't find the words he needs because two years in the grave, I still have a hold on him.

> *(The* **LIBRARIAN** *points at photo in frame on wall.)*

LIBRARIAN. What's that?

PHOTOGRAPHER. She notices a photo of mine hanging behind him.

LIBRARIAN. That's a real nice shot.

HARDWARE STORE OWNER. Yes.

LIBRARIAN. She was talented.

HARDWARE STORE OWNER. Yes.

LIBRARIAN. I like how everyone's personality always comes through.

HARDWARE STORE OWNER. Yeah.

LIBRARIAN. And the personality of the buildings too.

HARDWARE STORE OWNER. Yeah.

LIBRARIAN. They all feel alive.

PHOTOGRAPHER. Even now that I'm dead. But she doesn't say that. She shouldn't have pointed out the photograph.

LIBRARIAN. So dumb.

PHOTOGRAPHER. She thinks of leaving the store, the state, the country. Instead she walks towards the fear. Steels herself. And she says –

LIBRARIAN. I was going to – tomorrow are you – might you want to have dinner with me?

HARDWARE STORE OWNER. Oh. You mean?

LIBRARIAN. The new Italian place? Just dinner.

HARDWARE STORE OWNER. I know but –

PHOTOGRAPHER. In the silence, everything they can't say is said.

    (Light shift.)

HARDWARE STORE OWNER. I can't disrespect her memory. No matter what you think, it was love.

LIBRARIAN. There has never been anyone but you. Not really. Not anyone.

HARDWARE STORE OWNER. It wouldn't be right. Even if it's only dinner.

LIBRARIAN. I feel terrible but I was a little happy, just a little happy when I heard she died. I felt bad right after, but for a second –

    (Light shift.)

HARDWARE STORE OWNER. I'm sorry. I can't. It wouldn't be – not that – things are just really busy now. Maybe another time.

LIBRARIAN. Sure. Of course.

HARDWARE STORE OWNER. Busy.

LIBRARIAN. Busy. That's fine. I just thought –

HARDWARE STORE OWNER. Another time.

PHOTOGRAPHER. The Librarian leaves, trying to not let him see her face.

> *(The* **LIBRARIAN** *exits.)*

HARDWARE STORE OWNER. Wait! Your light bulbs.

PHOTOGRAPHER. But she has gone. I stay. I stay. He cannot see me but I stay. It hurts me to look at him but I stay, even as his edges blur. I stay.

Scene Ten
The Gravedigger

(Projected: the graveyard. The **GRAVEDIGGER**
digs with a shovel.)

PHOTOGRAPHER. The Gravedigger digs. The rain starts. The
Gravedigger digs. It rains harder.

It rains. It rains. It rains. The Gravedigger digs. It rains.
Rain. Rain.

*(We see all the characters look up as it rains
down.* **LIBRARIAN** *looks up and out.* **HARDWARE
STORE OWNER** *looks at the rain from inside.)*

(Blackout.)

*(Note: this play works best without an
intermission. However, if you absolutely need
one, it should go here.)*

ACT II

Scene One
The Photographer

(The **PHOTOGRAPHER** *onstage alone.)*

PHOTOGRAPHER. The rain stops eventually. It always does if you wait around long enough. I've become more patient. I've found peace by staying put. I look at the photographs and I –

(Sees audience.)

How about you? Everyone okay?

(Takes a few shots of audience which go up on the wall.)

This can be your Christmas card. I like that. That's a good color on you. Did you two come together? I'm glad you came to visit. Am I showing you everything you want to see? What next? I mustn't disappoint you. Or maybe disappointment is important too. Don't you think? Okay. The Perfume Maker.

Scene Two
The Perfume Maker

(Projected: interior of the **PERFUME MAKER'S** *lab. The* **PERFUME MAKER** *works. The* **PHOTOGRAPHER** *watches him.)*

PHOTOGRAPHER. The Perfume Maker works. He forgets to eat. He forgets to sleep. Somewhere is the perfect combination that will amplify the essence of the Waitress. With chemistry he will create a super version of her, so subtle yet hits you like a left hook after she walks away. If only he can figure it out.

PERFUME MAKER. Almost. No. What if –

PHOTOGRAPHER. The Perfume Maker works with a chemical fervor that drives him days past his natural stopping point. He is fueled by possibility.

PERFUME MAKER. Maybe – or – no.

PHOTOGRAPHER. He continues. Outside the Florist knocks on his door. He does not answer.

> (**FLORIST** *knocks.*)

FLORIST. Hello! It's me! It's just me. Hello! Hello! Hello! Hello!

PHOTOGRAPHER. The Florist leaves to open her flower shop.

> (**FLORIST** *exits.*)

I wonder about work and about the difference between a calling and a job. About what we want and what we think we want. And what we think we should want. I wonder about if we can ever know if we're doing good or just what feels good. I wonder if love is really the opposite of war or if it's a different kind of war. Is loving someone else something we invented so we could feel pain more intensely or is it us really trying to be happy? Why do we think the goal is happiness? Maybe it should be learning to live with misery. But no, I still believe it. I think we should try to be happy. Right? Sorry. Where were we?

Scene Three
The Florist and the Gravedigger

(Projected: interior of the flower shop. The **FLORIST** *is there waiting on the* **GRAVEDIGGER.***)*

PHOTOGRAPHER. The Gravedigger selects flowers.

GRAVEDIGGER. Yeah, like that except prettier.

FLORIST. Don't you just want the discards? For the graves?

GRAVEDIGGER. Today, I will buy some. I will spend money. Maybe I will spend a lot of money. Are they expensive?

FLORIST. Depends what you want and what you think expensive means.

GRAVEDIGGER. I have some money saved.

PHOTOGRAPHER. The Florist does not know what this means.

FLORIST. Is this for a grave?

GRAVEDIGGER. Yes. No.

FLORIST. Because I donate them to you for the graves. I support what you do. It makes me feel better to give them to you.

GRAVEDIGGER. I like flowers.

FLORIST. Look, you don't have to pay me. I'll give you the ones that won't last much longer, just like I always do.

GRAVEDIGGER. This time is different. I want to buy the most beautiful flowers you have. Which ones are those?

FLORIST. We all can't agree on that. If we all could agree on that, well, it would be a different world.

GRAVEDIGGER. Which do you like best?

FLORIST. It doesn't matter what I think.

GRAVEDIGGER. You're a woman. You might know.

FLORIST. You're buying them for someone special?

GRAVEDIGGER. Never mind that. Just tell me which ones. The most beautiful ones.

FLORIST. I don't feel like it's my place to say what someone else would like or wouldn't like. I know what I like.

FLORIST. Why don't you get what you like? And she'll know you better by it.

GRAVEDIGGER. I want to get what she likes.

FLORIST. Of course.

GRAVEDIGGER. She did say – do you have ponies?

FLORIST. No.

GRAVEDIGGER. It's just – how can she let go until I do? I have to show her. And she's stuck around longer than most but I see her fading. I know the signs. It won't be long now. Whether she wants to or not. So... Flowers like that.

FLORIST. Uh.

PHOTOGRAPHER. Then he sees me.

GRAVEDIGGER. Shh. Act normal.

FLORIST. How am I acting?

PHOTOGRAPHER. (*To* GRAVEDIGGER.) Hi.

GRAVEDIGGER. (*Looking down.*) I'm just getting some flowers, like I always do.

PHOTOGRAPHER. Don't go out of your way on my account.

GRAVEDIGGER. Just getting some flowers.

FLORIST. What's happening?

GRAVEDIGGER. I don't want to embarrass anyone.

FLORIST. Okay. I can support that.

GRAVEDIGGER. But I want the biggest most beautiful bouquet you can make. Use all the flowers that mean nice things and that smell good. Put all the pretty ones together that look prettier next to each other.

FLORIST. Okay.

GRAVEDIGGER. It's important.

FLORIST. Okay.

PHOTOGRAPHER. Is that for me?

GRAVEDIGGER. It's to say goodbye and all of the other things I want to say but can't. Because.

PHOTOGRAPHER. Goodbye?

FLORIST. A goodbye bouquet. Got it.

(The **FLORIST** *makes an elaborate bouquet.*
The **PHOTOGRAPHER** *steps out.)*

PHOTOGRAPHER. Goodbye?

FLORIST. You like this?

PHOTOGRAPHER. It seems I'm on a time frame.

GRAVEDIGGER. Put the yellow ones in.

PHOTOGRAPHER. And that death does not take away one's ability to be moved. I'm feeling five distinct feelings. One. Two. Three...no. Just three. Let's move on.

FLORIST. How about more like this?

*(***PHOTOGRAPHER*** moves away. Lights go out*
on **FLORIST** *and* **GRAVEDIGGER** *who exit.)*

PHOTOGRAPHER. I need a minute. I'm sorry. I just need to stop for a minute. Maybe. Here are. Here are some photos I took.

(Projected: the town and inhabitants of the
town. The **PHOTOGRAPHER** *collects herself.*
Note: If you're not doing projections, you can
do a slide show of blank slides or hand out an
album of photos as one production did.)

PHOTOGRAPHER. Okay. That's good. Where were we?

Scene Four
The Young Woman and the Young Man

(Projected: the Town Green.)

PHOTOGRAPHER. The Town Green. It's beautiful, isn't it? Quaint, people say, if they're not from here. If you're from here, you may stop noticing. It takes effort to not stop noticing.

> *(***YOUNG MAN*** enters pulling a child's wagon full of books stacked up, bound together so they reach heights much higher than they otherwise would – almost as tall as the ***YOUNG MAN*** himself.* ***YOUNG WOMAN*** *enters from opposite direction.)*

YOUNG MAN. Florence, my love.

YOUNG WOMAN. Robert.

PHOTOGRAPHER. The Young Couple are engaged. Being engaged is a constant. For a short period of time you can say "my fiancé" this and "my fiancé" that. But sometimes you feel more engaged than other times because being engaged is not a constant.

YOUNG MAN. I'm getting closer, I think. To figuring it all out. This book maybe. Or this one. They all say a lot of things. About how to be. Some of them you have to decode. Some are hard to understand or are not directly applicable. But then if you read the next book, sometimes you start to understand the previous book. Sometimes they don't make any sense for pages and pages. Sometimes I fall asleep. But this is important. I'm going to figure it all out.

PHOTOGRAPHER. The Young Woman doesn't know what to say or how to say it.

YOUNG WOMAN. Robert.

PHOTOGRAPHER. She says.

YOUNG WOMAN. Robert. I – if – when – I –

YOUNG MAN. What's that?

PHOTOGRAPHER. The Young Woman feels the heavy weight increase, the weight she has been feeling ever since –

(**YOUNG WOMAN** *collapses.*)

YOUNG MAN. Florence! Are you okay? Help! Help! Hey! Someone!

(**EMT 1** *and* **EMT 2** *arrive and go to work. They revive her.*)

EMT 1. Stand back.

EMT 2. Did she complain of any pain?

EMT 1. What did she have for breakfast?

EMT 2. Miss? Young Woman, can you hear me?

YOUNG WOMAN. Yes. Sorry. Sorry, everyone.

YOUNG MAN. What's wrong?

EMT 2. Are you okay to sit up?

EMT 1. Drink this.

YOUNG WOMAN. Thank you. I'm fine. I just – I can't do it, Robert.

YOUNG MAN. What?

YOUNG WOMAN. I can't marry you.

EMT 1 & EMT 2. Ohh.

YOUNG MAN. But our love. These books. That ring.

YOUNG WOMAN. I just don't think I can be someone's wife. When you asked, I was so happy, but then the other stuff came. Not just doubt. Not just fear. Dread. I felt so lonely. So very lonely. And trapped.

YOUNG MAN. No.

YOUNG WOMAN. I'm not ready to be in a marriage.

YOUNG MAN. But our love.

YOUNG WOMAN. It is a real thing. But for how long? I am not who I will be. Neither are you. We change. We evolve. Marriage will not solve this.

EMT 1. We've seen this before. My first husband.

EMT 2. My second wife.

YOUNG MAN. But we can change together.

YOUNG WOMAN. I just can't now.

YOUNG MAN. We will be different than the rest. We will try harder. We will always be kind.

YOUNG WOMAN. There is nothing you can say.

(**YOUNG WOMAN** *gives him the engagement ring back.* **YOUNG MAN** *accepts it.*)

YOUNG MAN. I'm going to read the books anyway. So when it comes, I'll be ready. I'll wait for you.

YOUNG WOMAN. I don't know if it's fair to you. But then again. I could let you get away and always regret it.

YOUNG MAN. Oh.

YOUNG WOMAN. Are you hungry? Let's have a meal and see where it goes.

YOUNG MAN. I think I need to be alone. Right now. Call me tomorrow.

YOUNG WOMAN. Okay.

YOUNG MAN. Or the day after. Or the day after that. I have a lot of reading to do. I might need different books.

YOUNG WOMAN. Will you answer the phone when I call?

YOUNG MAN. I don't know.

(**YOUNG MAN** *and* **YOUNG WOMAN** *exit in different directions.*)

EMT 2. Too bad.

EMT 1. Yup.

(**EMT 1** *and* **EMT 2** *start to exit. They are offstage or almost offstage for their next lines.*)

PHOTOGRAPHER. So, that's sad.

EMT 2. You still with that guy?

EMT 1. Yup.

Scene Five
The Librarian and the Photographer

(Projected: the graveyard. The **LIBRARIAN** *walks to the grave of The* **PHOTOGRAPHER**. *The* **PHOTOGRAPHER** *watches.)*

PHOTOGRAPHER. She – this... So this is happening. At my grave. The Librarian.

LIBRARIAN. Hi. This is weird. Hi. I wanted to... I saw Charlie. I went to see Charlie, I mean. Wow. This is hard. I. Well, I guess I came for your blessing? I know we were never what you'd call the best of friends. Not that we – I don't have any animosity. I understood. I wanted good things for you. Better than what happened. I mean that. I'm not bitter. I'm resigned. I have my tea. I have my books. I'm not complaining. I don't want an exciting life. But that's not what I came to say. It's been a long time. When I let him go all those years ago. I guess what I'm saying is, I want him back. Which is to say get to know who he has become. But I can't do that if I don't feel like it's okay with you. I've come to you to formally make peace so that he and I – what am I saying? He doesn't want me. He has his own life. His own ways. It can't work. And he doesn't need more love. The love you had was enough for life. Wasn't it? I'm sorry to bother you. Please rest. Peacefully. Sorry.

*(***GRAVEDIGGER** *has entered during this. He has arms full of flowers.)*

GRAVEDIGGER. Renee.

LIBRARIAN. Hi Earl. How's your mother?

GRAVEDIGGER. Good. Good. She crochets now.

LIBRARIAN. It's good to stay busy.

GRAVEDIGGER. Is it?

LIBRARIAN. When you came in, did you hear me, talking to the gravestone?

GRAVEDIGGER. Oh. Eh. Um. Yup. Yup.

LIBRARIAN. It's silly I know. She can't hear me.

GRAVEDIGGER. She can hear you. She hears you all right. Yeah. Yup. The question isn't whether she can hear you. The question is if – when she'll –

PHOTOGRAPHER. Stop.

> (*The* **GRAVEDIGGER** *stops speaking.* **PHOTOGRAPHER** *exits, plunging them into darkness and walking into her own light and towards the next scene.*)

Scene Six
The Perfume Maker

(Projected: interior of the **PERFUME MAKER**'s *lab. The* **PHOTOGRAPHER** *speaks to us.)*

PHOTOGRAPHER. Look. I just record things. Okay? Don't ask me to... I mean. Look. I'm a person too. I may not be – look, I just. Don't judge me. Give me a break. You're on my side, aren't you? Okay. Well. And then. And then the Perfume Maker has a eureka moment.

PERFUME MAKER. Eureka!

PHOTOGRAPHER. He smells the perfume and he knows he has created perfection.

PERFUME MAKER. It is her, but more. She will smell wonderful. And the diner smells will not harm it. And her sweat will feed it. And she will smell it and she will know. She will know.

PHOTOGRAPHER. What will she know?

PERFUME MAKER. Everything.

PHOTOGRAPHER. He never stops to think if this is a good idea. He does not understand the mystery of people or love or affection. He knows he can do this one thing and he knows she is special. So he does the thing he can do for the special woman. And then –

PERFUME MAKER. And then –

PHOTOGRAPHER. Well... Whatever comes after that. He prepares the bottle of perfume.

> *(***PERFUME MAKER*** does so. His lab fades away. The* **GRAVEDIGGER** *approaches, carrying the bouquet of flowers. He tries to give them to her but she backs away.)*

GRAVEDIGGER. We have to talk.

PHOTOGRAPHER. Not now. I can't! You can't be here. Later. We'll talk later and figure it all out.

GRAVEDIGGER. But –

PHOTOGRAPHER. Later!

GRAVEDIGGER. You have to –

PHOTOGRAPHER. LATER!

*(The **GRAVEDIGGER** exits with the bouquet.)*

Scene Seven
The Waitress and the Policeman
and the Perfume Maker and the Florist

(Projected: interior of the diner. The **WAITRESS** *is waiting on the* **POLICEMAN** *who is seated.)*

PHOTOGRAPHER. At the diner. The Waitress feels the special chemicals her body creates each time the Policeman comes into the diner.

WAITRESS. What can I get you?

POLICEMAN. What are the specials?

WAITRESS. Well, those aren't on the menu. You know that.

POLICEMAN. Oh you mean the special specials.

PHOTOGRAPHER. She flirts her best flirt. He smiles back. She refills his coffee. He looks at her. She feels him look at her.

POLICEMAN. I'll have the meatloaf sandwich.

WAITRESS. Of course. You want anything special with that?

POLICEMAN. Special or special special?

WAITRESS. Well...

POLICEMAN. Surprise me.

(The **WAITRESS** *moves away, behind the counter or to the kitchen.)*

PHOTOGRAPHER. She wishes she knew how to surprise him. How to surprise herself. Should she make a move maybe? Or wait for him to make a move. But what if he never does?

WAITRESS. Today –

PHOTOGRAPHER. She thinks.

WAITRESS. Today I will be bold.

PHOTOGRAPHER. But she does not stop to think what this means. It will take care of itself, perhaps. The Policeman thinks about garden gnomes.

POLICEMAN. I don't understand why. You got a nice garden. Some bushes. Some flowers, that stuff and then you get a plastic, rubber, ceramic gnome? What for?

PHOTOGRAPHER. He puzzles over this. He drinks his coffee.

POLICEMAN. And now fairies too. And fairy houses. Who knows what? I guess people like it. It makes them happy, I guess. Flamingoes. Hmm.

PHOTOGRAPHER. He thinks about the vandalism behind the school.

POLICEMAN. Why you want to go and do that?

PHOTOGRAPHER. The complicated nature of being human sometimes confounds the Policeman. The Perfume Maker walks through the door.

> (*The* **POLICEMAN** *and the* **WAITRESS** *look up as he enters and then away. The* **PERFUME MAKER** *sits at another table.*)

The Perfume Maker does not know what to do. He thinks about getting up, thrusting the bottle in the Waitress's hands and then running out. But he stays seated. The opportunity maybe will present itself. He is buzzing with anticipation. He simply cannot wait for the moment.

> (*The* **WAITRESS** *comes to The* **PERFUME MAKER**'s *table and pours him coffee.*)

PERFUME MAKER. Nice day.

WAITRESS. (*Not unfriendly.*) It's okay. The usual?

PERFUME MAKER. Yes. No. Today is different.

WAITRESS. Is it? Haven't seen you in a few days.

PERFUME MAKER. Been busy.

WAITRESS. It's good to stay busy.

PERFUME MAKER. I was making something.

PHOTOGRAPHER. It is at this point the Waitress feels an anxiety she cannot name. Nor does she know its cause.

WAITRESS. Oh, do you make things, Martin?

PHOTOGRAPHER. – She asks and immediately feels like she opened a jar she should not have opened.

PERFUME MAKER. I make perfume.

PHOTOGRAPHER. This is not what she expects him to say.

PERFUME MAKER. In fact,

PHOTOGRAPHER. He tries to laugh. What a lark. How casual it all is.

PERFUME MAKER. I made a perfume for you.

PHOTOGRAPHER. He fumbles with the bottle but finally places it in her hand.

>   (**WAITRESS** *accepts the bottle.*)

WAITRESS. Oh.

PERFUME MAKER. It's not a big deal.

PHOTOGRAPHER. The Waitress feels like someone just handed her a bomb.

WAITRESS. I don't want it! I mean, you shouldn't have.

PERFUME MAKER. It was no trouble.

WAITRESS. I can't accept this.

PERFUME MAKER. It's nothing.

WAITRESS. I wish you hadn't done this. *(Softening, guilty.)* You made it for me?

PERFUME MAKER. No. I mean, yes. It fits your scent profile.

WAITRESS. My what?

PERFUME MAKER. Your scent –

PHOTOGRAPHER. He feels suddenly dirty. Filthy. He sweats. He stinks and it's a stink no scent can cover up.

WAITRESS. I see. Right. Well. Right.

PHOTOGRAPHER. She doesn't feel threatened exactly but she doesn't want to owe him. Can she kick him out? But that seems mean. And unprovoked.

WAITRESS. What am I getting you? The usual?

PERFUME MAKER. I have to go.

>   (*The* **PERFUME MAKER** *stands and quickly exits the diner. On his way out he almost walks into the* **FLORIST** *who carries flowers.*)

FLORIST. *(Surprise.)* Martin!

PERFUME MAKER. Not now. Not now! Will you just – get out of the way?!

(PERFUME MAKER pushes by FLORIST who drops the flowers. She leaves them there. He exits.)

PHOTOGRAPHER. The Florist sees clearly that no amount of perseverance will ever work. The sadness fills her. More sadness. More than she can bear. It fills to the top. She takes a breath. And then another. One more. Then, her natural optimism catches up. She realizes she is free now. And tomorrow something new. Maybe. Someone new.

FLORIST. Okay!

(The FLORIST exits. The WAITRESS is having a hard time.)

PHOTOGRAPHER. The Waitress wonders if she should quit her job. She can't bear the thought of seeing the Perfume Maker tomorrow. Perhaps it's time to move on. Instead she opens the perfume and dabs a bit on her wrists and behind her ear.

(She does this.)

It smells good. But it's nothing special, she thinks. Here is what will happen. She will continue to wear the perfume. The Perfume Maker will notice this when he comes back the next day. Neither of them will mention it. They will pretend nothing has happened. He will order the usual. She will get it for him. Maybe the quality of small talk is just a little better. But otherwise, life goes on for the living. Right now, the Policeman is wondering about his meatloaf sandwich.

POLICEMAN. Jen?

(The WAITRESS brings the meatloaf sandwich over to the POLICEMAN.)

WAITRESS. Here you are.

POLICEMAN. Much obliged.

PHOTOGRAPHER. The Policeman does not know why but he suddenly looks at the Waitress in a new light. She is beautiful. How did he never see it before? She is charismatic and strong and she contains multitudes. And she smells so good.

(The **WAITRESS** *starts to leave the table.)*

POLICEMAN. Hold on. About that special. When do you get off?

WAITRESS. Oh. You mean –

POLICEMAN. Can I buy you a drink? Or dinner?

WAITRESS. Dinner would be nice.

PHOTOGRAPHER. And dinner is nice. Many many more dinners follow. But that's a different story.

Scene Eight
The History Professor and the Mystery Novelist

(Projected: Harry's Place. The **PHOTOGRAPHER** *walks into the next scene. The* **HISTORY PROFESSOR** *and The* **MYSTERY NOVELIST** *enter while* **PHOTOGRAPHER** *speaks and they sit at a table.)*

PHOTOGRAPHER. The History Professor and the Mystery Novelist sit in silence. They have been sitting for quite a while. Hours? It feels like hours. I'm not good with time any more. It's probably not hours. They sit. They sit. They sit more. One of them will have to say it. Neither wants to be the first.

HISTORY PROFESSOR. *(Noise of clearing throat.)* Ahem.

MYSTERY NOVELIST. What's that?

HISTORY PROFESSOR. Just clearing my throat.

MYSTERY NOVELIST. Oh. I thought you were going to say something.

HISTORY PROFESSOR. No.

MYSTERY NOVELIST. Me either.

(Pause.)

Beautiful day.

HISTORY PROFESSOR. It's really temperate.

MYSTERY NOVELIST. How are things?

HISTORY PROFESSOR. Oh, you know. Okay.

MYSTERY NOVELIST. Me too.

PHOTOGRAPHER. They miss each other with an ache more painful than when they were first dating. They are both miserable. But he doesn't think she feels the same way. She does. She thinks he's screwing his teaching assistant. He isn't. He thinks she loves her empty house. She did. For a day or two. She thinks he loves his bachelor life. He doesn't. They are so desperate it's acidic in their mouths.

HISTORY PROFESSOR. How's the house?

MYSTERY NOVELIST. Good. Good.

HISTORY PROFESSOR. If you want, I could come over, take care of some chores. Change a few light bulbs.

MYSTERY NOVELIST. That would be nice. If it's not too much trouble. I'm sure you got a lot going on.

HISTORY PROFESSOR. I wouldn't want to intrude.

MYSTERY NOVELIST. It would be nice.

HISTORY PROFESSOR. If you want. Just for a few minutes. I don't have to stay long if you don't want.

MYSTERY NOVELIST. It's quiet in the house.

HISTORY PROFESSOR. You like it like that.

MYSTERY NOVELIST. I do. Sometimes.

PHOTOGRAPHER. He thinks about the red couch. He thinks about her. He thinks about her on the red couch. He sighs. She doesn't recognize this sigh. She thinks he is impatient to get away.

MYSTERY NOVELIST. Sorry if I'm keeping you.

HISTORY PROFESSOR. Not at all. How's the novel?

MYSTERY NOVELIST. Getting there. How's the research?

HISTORY PROFESSOR. Frustrating.

(*Beat.*)

I miss you.

PHOTOGRAPHER. She didn't expect that.

MYSTERY NOVELIST. You do? What do you miss?

HISTORY PROFESSOR. Everything.

PHOTOGRAPHER. And he means it. She thinks she might miss everything about him too. Almost everything? Everything. Last night she found his fingernail clipping on the rug and almost cried. But she doesn't say that. Instead she says –

MYSTERY NOVELIST. You can move back in if you want.

PHOTOGRAPHER. She surprises herself by saying this.

HISTORY PROFESSOR. I'd like that. Do you mean –?

MYSTERY NOVELIST. On a trial basis.

HISTORY PROFESSOR. Yes.

MYSTERY NOVELIST. We try. Again. Us.

HISTORY PROFESSOR. We. Our marriage?

MYSTERY NOVELIST. Our life. Are you in agreement?

HISTORY PROFESSOR. I am.

MYSTERY NOVELIST. What will we tell the children?

HISTORY PROFESSOR. We'll think of something.

(They kiss.)

MYSTERY NOVELIST. Okay then.

HISTORY PROFESSOR. Right.

MYSTERY NOVELIST. I'm glad.

HISTORY PROFESSOR. I am too.

MYSTERY NOVELIST. We should come here more.

PHOTOGRAPHER. Of course, it's a seasonal restaurant. And the season is almost over. A cold wind blows in. The first of the leaves turn and fall from the trees. The maples always succumb first.

Scene Nine
The Photographer and the Gravedigger

(Projected: the graveyard. The **PHOTOGRAPHER** *finds herself there.* **GRAVEDIGGER** *appears. He holds the bouquet of flowers, larger now because he has also picked up the flowers that the* **FLORIST** *dropped.)*

GRAVEDIGGER. It's time now.

PHOTOGRAPHER. Time?

GRAVEDIGGER. It's time to go –

PHOTOGRAPHER. But I have – there are so many –

GRAVEDIGGER. When it's time, it's time. You can feel it, can't you?

PHOTOGRAPHER. But I can't. I'm not ready.

GRAVEDIGGER. You can't argue with me about it. I mean it won't do any good. When it's time, it's time.

PHOTOGRAPHER. I won't do it.

GRAVEDIGGER. You're fading.

PHOTOGRAPHER. I know.

GRAVEDIGGER. You've stuck around a while. They don't usually. But you're different.

(He hands her the flowers. She accepts them.)

PHOTOGRAPHER. Thank you, Earl, for...everything.

GRAVEDIGGER. It was nothing.

(The **PHOTOGRAPHER** *kisses him on the cheek.)*

PHOTOGRAPHER. There's just one thing I have to do.

(The **GRAVEDIGGER** *looks at her but says nothing. The projection changes. He leaves.)*

Scene Ten
The Photographer and the Hardware Store Owner and the Librarian

> (*Projected: the hardware store. The* **PHOTOGRAPHER** *among the audience gives out flowers.*)

PHOTOGRAPHER. I hope you have someone like Earl someday. If it's necessary. Should it be necessary.

> (*The mirrored ball drops from the ceiling. Light change. Music. The* **HARDWARE STORE OWNER** *and the* **LIBRARIAN** *dance close.*)

> (*Reacting to the flashback.*)

OH!

LIBRARIAN. Promise me we'll be together forever.

HARDWARE STORE OWNER. That's quite a promise.

LIBRARIAN. But that's easy. We have love.

HARDWARE STORE OWNER. We do. Okay. I promise.

LIBRARIAN. We'll be together forever?

HARDWARE STORE OWNER. We'll be together forever.

LIBRARIAN. Even in death?

HARDWARE STORE OWNER. What?

LIBRARIAN. If I die, you'll keep loving me and never love anyone else.

HARDWARE STORE OWNER. Okay.

LIBRARIAN. Until we are buried next to each other.

HARDWARE STORE OWNER. This is getting morbid.

LIBRARIAN. Just tell me you love me forever and always.

HARDWARE STORE OWNER. I do.

> (*The* **PHOTOGRAPHER** *has given all her flowers away except for one. She gives this to the* **LIBRARIAN** *now. The lights change. The music changes. The* **LIBRARIAN** *and the* **HARDWARE STORE OWNER** *separate and he begins to*

dance with the **PHOTOGRAPHER**. *They are all older now. The* **LIBRARIAN** *moves outside and watches them through the hardware store window.)*

HARDWARE STORE OWNER. Suzanne.

PHOTOGRAPHER. Charlie.

HARDWARE STORE OWNER. I knew you were still here. Somehow.

PHOTOGRAPHER. I never wanted to leave you. You know that.

HARDWARE STORE OWNER. I miss you so much it hurts.

PHOTOGRAPHER. Me too, Charlie. Me too.

HARDWARE STORE OWNER. Some days, now, I wonder what for. With you it was bearable, but now –

PHOTOGRAPHER. You got to find your own reasons. Please. I want to know, when I'm gone, you'll be okay.

HARDWARE STORE OWNER. Don't go.

PHOTOGRAPHER. I want you – I want you to go to her.

HARDWARE STORE OWNER. No.

PHOTOGRAPHER. It's what I want. And what you want too. You're alive. Be alive.

HARDWARE STORE OWNER. I forgot how.

PHOTOGRAPHER. You'll pick it back up.

HARDWARE STORE OWNER. *(Starting to come around.)* What if... What if I do it all wrong?

PHOTOGRAPHER. You can't do nothing new and wonder why you're unhappy with your life.

HARDWARE STORE OWNER. *(Accepting.)* I know.

PHOTOGRAPHER. Bye, Charlie.

HARDWARE STORE OWNER. This doesn't mean I'll forget you.

PHOTOGRAPHER. Goodbye.

(She kisses him, moves away. The lights become normal daytime lights. The **LIBRARIAN** *has re-entered. We are in the hardware store and the* **LIBRARIAN** *and the*

HARDWARE STORE OWNER *look at each other. Some time has passed but no time has passed.)*

HARDWARE STORE OWNER. I was wondering when I'd see you again.

LIBRARIAN. I forgot the light bulbs.

HARDWARE STORE OWNER. I'm glad you came back.

LIBRARIAN. You are?

HARDWARE STORE OWNER. I was thinking about that dinner.

LIBRARIAN. Oh.

HARDWARE STORE OWNER. I think. I think. I'd really like that. To take you out.

LIBRARIAN. Aren't we too busy?

HARDWARE STORE OWNER. No. We aren't. Unless you don't want to.

LIBRARIAN. I'd like that.

HARDWARE STORE OWNER. It's been a long time. You're more beautiful now.

LIBRARIAN. No.

HARDWARE STORE OWNER. It's true.

(He takes her hand and they exit. The **PHOTOGRAPHER** *reappears. All the projections we have seen in the play so far flash on the screen super fast, one after another. The* **PHOTOGRAPHER** *takes her camera off and places it at her feet.)*

PHOTOGRAPHER. So that's that. It was really nice showing you around. I hope it helped. I only wish we had more time. But I guess... Okay. Then. I guess... I have loved.

(Projection: a blank slide – all white light. The lights come up big and full. As bright and as white as possible. It blinds the audience. It envelops the **PHOTOGRAPHER.** *She raises her arms and looks up. And then blackout.)*

End of Play